What Are You So Grumpy About?

by

TOM LICHTENHELD

DID YOUR MOM and DAD FORGET TO BUY YOUR KIND OF CEREAL,

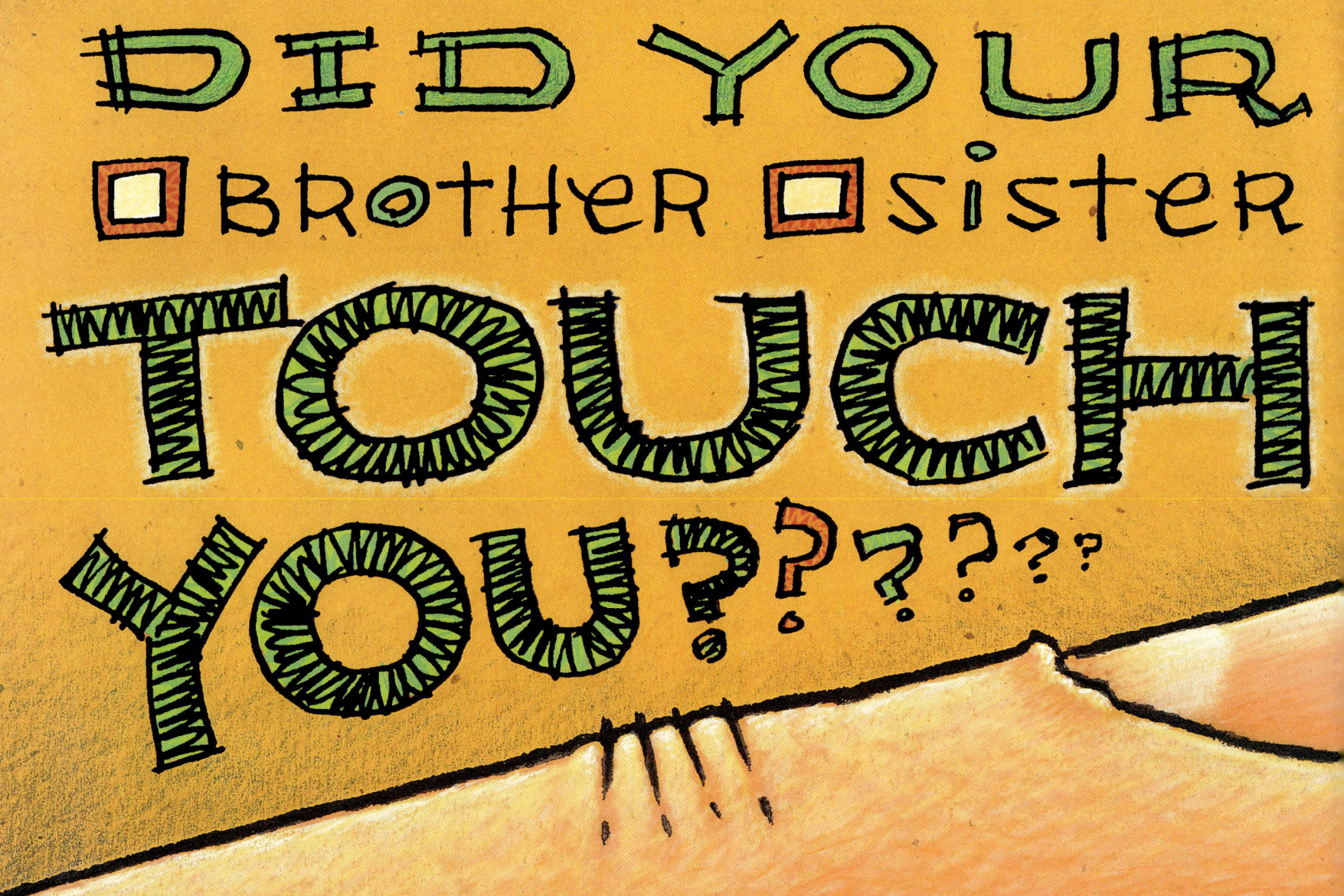

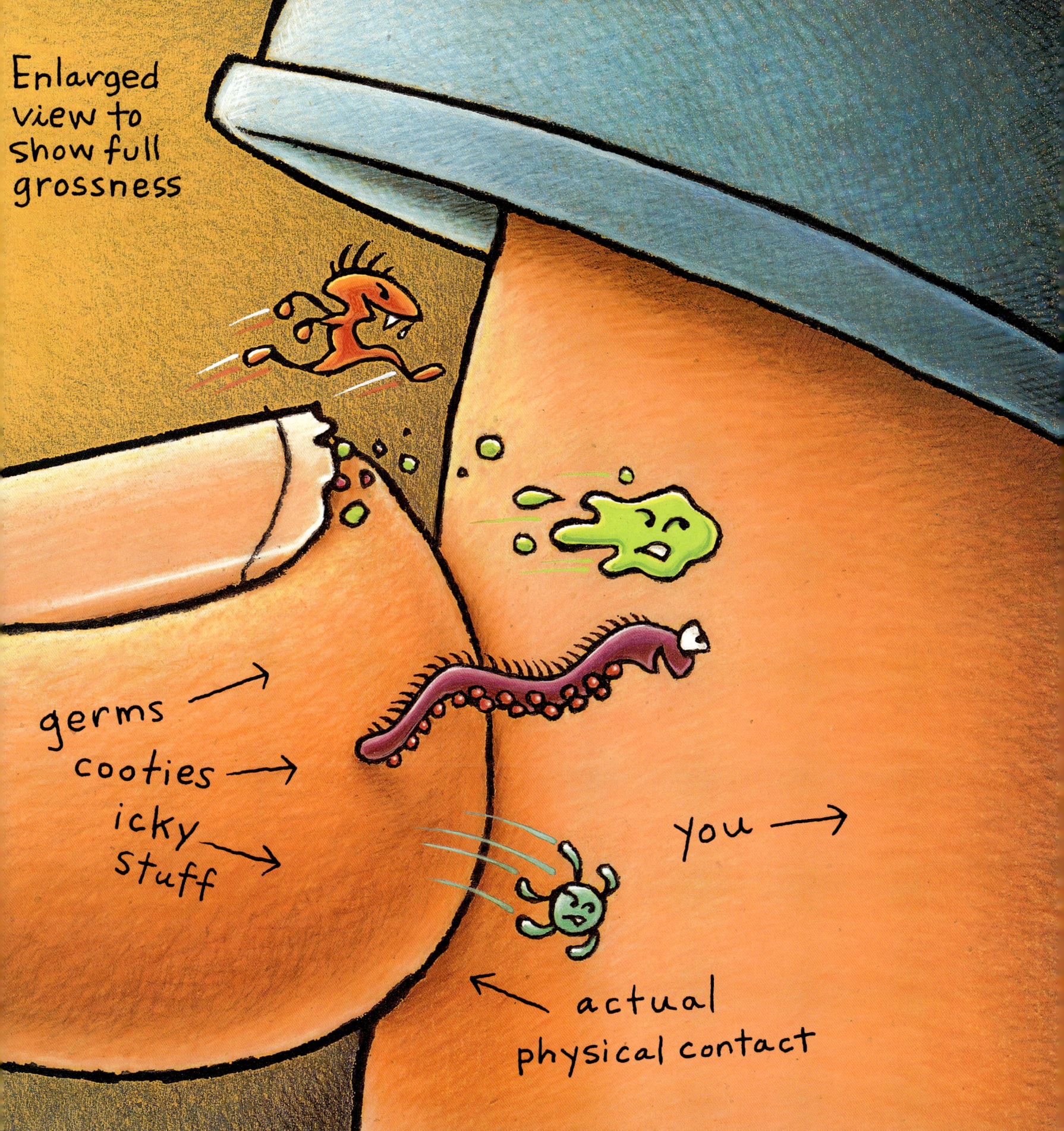

ub your toe?

Did you have to pick up your room?

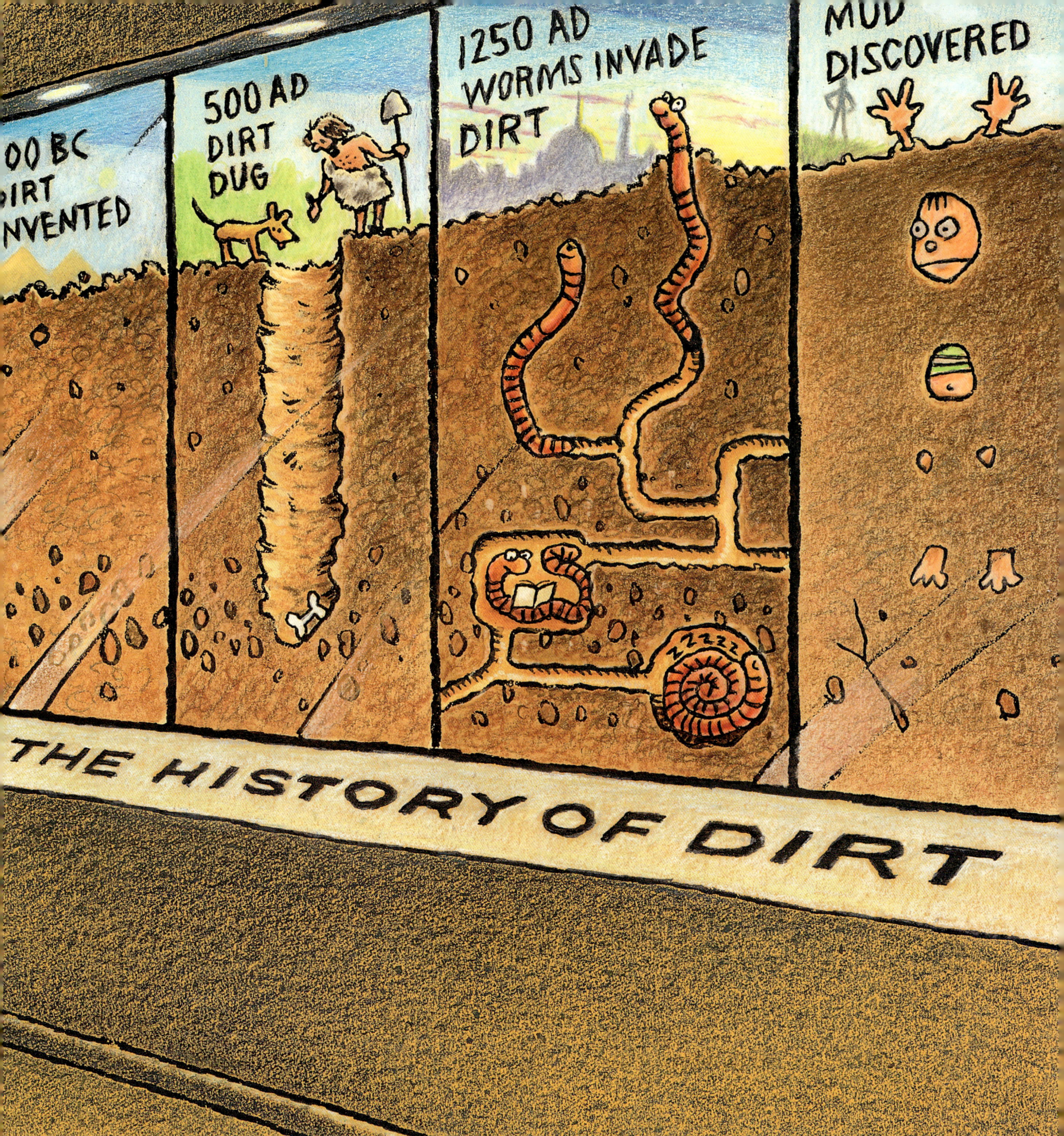

DID YOUR RELATIVES COME OVER and YOUR GRANDMA GAVE YOU A BIG HUG?

STUFF HAPPENS, PEOPLE AMAZED
More inside

Dai

BOY LOST BOSOM!

SEARCH PARTY HEARS VOICE — REMAINS HOPEFUL

DeKalb, Ill. — Little Bobby Yablonski disappeared Sunday afternoon, following an exuberant greeting from his grandmother, Reba Gillett. "I had just tousled his hair and pinched his cheek," gasped a surprised Ms. Gillett, "then I gave him a bear hug, and poof! — he was gone!" Friends of the fa

mother is confident he'll return soon. "He always comes home by the time the streetlights come on," she explained. Meanwhile, Grandma has offered a reward to anyone with information leading to Bobby's return: twenty-five dollars and a l

Or the worst...

This book is dedicated to my friends at Fallon,
who were never grumpy and who always inspired me.

Thanks to my wife, Jan, for making it all happen.

Copyright © 2003 by Tom Lichtenheld

All rights reserved. No part of this book may be reproduced in any form
or by any electronic or mechanical means, including information storage
and retrieval systems, without permission in writing from the publisher, except
by a reviewer who may quote brief passages in a review.

First Edition

Library of Congress Cataloging-in-Publication Data
Lichtenheld, Tom.
What are you so grumpy about? / Tom Lichtenheld. — 1st ed.
p.cm.
Summary: A collection of cartoons that present various reasons for being
grumpy, such as eating "grown-up" cereal, getting a boring birthday
present, doing chores, and being touched by your brother or sister.
ISBN 0-316-59236-6 (hc)
1. American wit and humor, Pictorial – Juvenile literature.
2. Children – Caricatures and cartoons. [1. Mood (Psychology) – Humor.
2. Cartoons and comics.] I. Title.
NC1429.L532 A4 2003
741.5'973 – dc21
2002022487

10 9 8 7 6 5 4 3

PHX

Printed in Hong Kong

The illustrations for this book were done in ink,
colored pencil, gouache, watercolor, peas, and gravy.
The text was set in Mrs. Eaves,
and the display type was handlettered.
Design by Tom Lichtenheld